COLIN DANN

The Animals of Farthing Wood

BBC BOOKS

Published by BBC Books,
a division of BBC Enterprises Limited,
Woodlands, 80 Wood Lane, London W12 0TT

First published 1993

The original books in the *Animals of Farthing
Wood* series are published by Reed Children's
Books and Random House Children's Books.

Reprinted 1993

Text © 1993 Colin Dann
Stills © 1993 EBU

ISBN 0 563 36438 6

Designed by Louise Millar

Set in Palatino by Goodfellow & Egan Ltd, Cambridge
Printed and bound in Belgium by Proost NV
Colour separation by Dot Graduations Ltd, Chelmsford
Cover printed in Belgium by Proost NV

Farthing Wood was being destroyed. Men were clearing the trees to build houses and roads. Day by day the animals who lived in the wood saw more of their homes disappear.

Badger, Kestrel and Weasel looked glumly at the spreading wasteland.

"How long d'you think, Badger," Weasel gulped, "before they reach us?"

"Not long, I fear," Badger answered grimly.

Kestrel, flying overhead, brought even worse news. "They've filled in the pond!" she called.

Owl was horrified. "Not Farthing Pond?"

"But where shall we go to drink?" said Badger.

"There's still the stream," Weasel said.

"We'd better go and look," said Badger.

They were in for a shock. A lengthy drought had all but dried the stream up. Some other animals were already there, lapping at the remaining puddles.

Fox arrived next. "Not too good, is it?" he said, staring at the muddy trickle.

"We've a real problem," Badger agreed. "There's no sign of any rain."

"This is an emergency. I reckon it calls for an Assembly," said Fox.

"Right, there's no time to lose," Badger said to the smaller animals. "We must all spread the word around. A meeting. In my chambers. At dusk."

They hurried off to find the other woodland dwellers.

At sunset the animals gathered at the meeting place. Mole arrived late, through a tunnel in the wall.

"Late as usual, I'm afraid," he said. "Sorry."

"Friends, we all know why we're here," Badger began. "Our homes are being destroyed. We have nowhere to drink. Is there any way out of our difficulties? Has anyone a suggestion?"

The animals pondered. In the silence they heard a rumble overhead. Part of the ceiling collapsed and suddenly Toad tumbled into their midst.

"Toad!" they cried. "Wherever have you been all this time?"

"I've been travelling," Toad croaked. "I was captured last spring at the pond and taken *such* a distance away. But I escaped and, ever since, I've been working my way back here to all of you and my pond –"

"Pond?" Owl interrupted. "It's been filled in!"

Toad fell back, stunned. "It can't be," he muttered.

"Gone completely," Fox said. "Farthing Wood is up against it. We all need to drink and –"

"I know just the place to go," Toad cried. "It's called White Deer Park. I came across it on my travels. It's a Nature Reserve specially for wild creatures. We'd be protected from danger there."

It sounded too good to be true. "What do you think, Fox?" Badger asked.

"What else can we do?" Fox answered.

"Then it's White Deer Park, everyone!" Badger cried.

There were cheers from Toad. Euphoria broke out amongst the Assembly.

But Hare had thought of a snag. "How can we weaker animals travel to this Park alongside our natural enemies? We wouldn't be safe."

"That's easily dealt with," said Badger. "Remember the ancient woodland promise – The Oath of Mutual Protection. It's a promise not to –"

"Frighten," said Fox.

"Or bully," said Owl.

"Or eat one another," Adder added.

Everyone had to swear the Oath. Then Toad was named as guide on the journey.

"And as leader," said Badger, "I nominate Fox. He's the obvious choice."

"Thank you, Badger," said Fox.

The excited animals hurried to the exit.

"Remember, everyone," Fox called to them. "We meet by the Great Oak at midnight tomorrow."

The Farthing Wood animals had to endure the roar and crash of machinery for one more day, but at last silence fell. In the darkness the animals, sad at heart, said farewell to their old home and hastened to the meeting place.

"Is everyone here?" Fox asked.

"No. Mole's missing," said Badger.

"We can't wait, you know," Fox warned. "We must go now."

Badger nodded. "You go on then. I'll find Mole and somehow we'll catch you up."

Badger eventually found Mole, under a mound of earth.

"I'm not coming! I'm too slow and . . . I'd hold you up," Mole said tearfully.

"Of course you're coming. I'm not leaving you behind," Badger replied. "I'll help you." Badger put down a paw and lifted Mole onto his shoulder. "Right, now we have to catch up with the others."

All the animals cheered as the latecomers arrived, and together they passed through the building site.

By dawn everyone was very tired. Kestrel found them a safe place to rest.

Many hours later the animals awoke, feeling hungry and thirsty. Mole was desperate to find worms.

"The marsh is the place," Owl told him. "The ground's soft there."

The animals enjoyed a long drink at the marsh, cooling themselves in the water. Mole dug up some juicy worms. Many of the smaller animals were still exhausted from their efforts during the night, Toad amongst them.

"I think we travelled too far yesterday, Fox," Badger remarked.

"Too fast for us small ones," said Toad. "Too slow for you."

The party moved on. Toad was so tired he dropped behind.

Suddenly Weasel thought she smelt smoke. Hare saw a red glow in the sky.

"FIRE!" Kestrel shrieked from the air.

Fox was frightened but knew he had to find Toad, their guide. He told Kestrel and Owl to lead them to safety. Then, steeling himself, he ran towards the fire.

"Toad! Toad!" Fox found the little animal in the dry grass.

"Fox, you came back for me!"

"Hurry, or we'll be burnt alive." Fox bent and gently picked up Toad in his mouth.

Mole also had been left behind. He was greedy and wanted more worms, and so had begun to dig again oblivious of the growing danger of the fire. He was abandoned as the others put the marsh between them and the fire, using water as a barrier.

Poor Mole, alone underground, was trapped. "Oh! If I don't burn to death, I'll drown," he wailed. "I'll never be greedy again. Never!" He sobbed himself to sleep.

Men arrived with their machines to douse the flames another human had caused by carelessly dropping a burning cigarette into the dry grass. The animals retreated to an island in the middle of the marsh.

As the soil cooled, Mole emerged. The earth was black. He thought his friends were dead.

"Alone, all alone," Mole wept bitterly. A firefighter saw him and lifted him to safety. Mole was tucked into a coat pocket.

The animals watched as the fire was extinguished. The fireman's coat was laid on the ground. Mole crawled from the pocket. His friends spotted him. While Owl and Kestrel distracted the men, Fox dashed to Mole's rescue.

At last the men left the scene. Mole and his friends were reunited.

"Where to now, Toad?" asked Fox.

"We make for the farmland," said Toad. "And what do you think? It's starting to rain!"

Moments later the animals found themselves in the midst of a thunderstorm. Toad loved it and danced about happily. But the others didn't and the voles and mice were soon up to their necks in mud. Even the larger animals were desperate to find shelter.

Toad led them on through an orchard to a barn. Inside they found straw. "Just the job for drying ourselves," declared a hedgehog.

Fox was worried by the open door, but the other animals were already making themselves comfortable, relieved to be out of the storm.

"Kestrel's keeping watch in a plum tree," Owl told Fox. "Pheasant will relieve her later."

Soon all were asleep. When it was Pheasant's turn to keep guard he wouldn't be disturbed. So his mate went in his place, but she fell asleep.

Meanwhile the farmer and his dog went to collect eggs. In the chicken coop they found a slaughter had taken place. The farmer was furious. "Foxes again!"

He turned to his dog. "Where were you, you useless cur?" He aimed a kick at the beast. The dog yelped.

Pheasant's mate heard the dog and was alarmed. "I'd better warn the others." She began to walk back. But the farmer had his gun trained on her. The animals in the barn heard gunshot.

They rushed to the door but it was closed with a slam. The farmer ordered his dog to guard the barn. "Keep them in there, Bruno, or else!" "Help! We're trapped!" cried Pheasant.

Fox said, "Check the
windows." They
were shut fast.
   "There's only one way out
of here," said Owl. "By digging!"
   "Who's the best tunneller?"
asked Fox.
   "Mole!" everyone cried.
   Mole was delighted. Then he saw
the floor. "I can't tunnel through wood," he wailed.
   "Never mind," said Squirrel. "There are plenty of us who
can gnaw."
   "Come on, everyone," called Weasel. And she sank her
teeth into the floor.
   The animals gnawed busily and soon a hole appeared in
the floor. Mole slipped through and began to tunnel. He
kicked the earth behind him. Soon the hole was big
enough for Badger.

Badger followed Mole, widening the tunnel as he went. Mole reached the orchard and tunnelled upward.

"Hurry, everybody! Into the tunnel," Fox ordered. He watched them disappear and brought up the rear himself.

Meanwhile the farmer had re-loaded his gun. He meant to settle a score with Fox. He tramped to the barn and flung the door open. The barn was empty. The man couldn't believe his eyes.

The animals were just in time. They broke into a run, as the furious farmer fired his gun into the tunnel.

In the orchard the farmer's dog had picked up the animals' scent. Barking angrily, it began to follow them.

"It's me he's after," Fox said grimly. "Badger, take the others ahead." Toad dismounted and Fox turned to confront his pursuer.

"So. You want me?"

"My master wants you dead," said the dog. "You killed his chickens."

"Not me. Wrong fox. Your master won't thank you for another mistake."

The dog hesitated. "Oh, I'm taking you back anyway," it growled.

"You'll have to kill me first, then. And the man won't like that either, since he wants to do it himself."

"You're so clever!" the dog barked.

Fox knew the dog was beaten. Turning, he coolly walked away. The dog glared at him, puzzled. But eventually, feeling foolish, it slunk off.

Toad was waiting. "You were wonderful, Fox!" he greeted him. "So cool. You really foxed him!" They laughed and hastened to catch up with the others.

The animals travelled on and arrived at a river. The smaller animals were afraid.

"Don't worry," said Toad. "I'll go first. I'm very small and if I can do it, so can you." He dived in and struck out for the far bank.

A little later they heard him calling. "I've made it! Come on, mateys!"

Fox lined up the rest of the party along the bank. "We'll all go together. Good luck!"

The animals entered the water. Kestrel and Owl flew across to join Toad. All went well until the rabbits, who were a nervous bunch, began to panic. Fox stayed with them, trying to calm them down.

The more he tried, the more they panicked. They were swimming in all directions. The other animals who by now had crossed safely, could see something was wrong.

"Look, Badger!" said Mole. "That mass of debris floating downstream. It's heading straight for Fox and the rabbits!"

"Quickly, my friends!" Badger cried. "We must save them!"

Badger swam straight for Fox, while other animals each selected a rabbit and steered it to safety. Fox was exhausted and could swim no more.

"Save yourself, Badger!" he pleaded.

But Badger refused. "I'm not leaving you," he said.

The debris struck them and carried them downstream. The animals ran along the bank, trying to keep them in view. Kestrel flew above.

"Can you see them?" they called to her.

"There's no sign of them," she answered.

Then Toad thought he saw something in the river. "Look!" he croaked.

Badger's striped head bobbed up among reeds, then immediately sank again.

"It's Badger!" Mole cried joyfully.

At once Toad, Weasel, Hedgehog and Hare dived to the rescue.

Together they freed Badger from the reeds and pushed him ashore.

"Where's Fox?" Badger gasped.

"We don't know," Hare answered.

Badger looked forlornly at the river.

Kestrel, who had followed Fox, had seen him lying across some driftwood. She flew closer. Fox wasn't moving. She followed him to a bridge and hovered while the debris drifted underneath.

The driftwood came through without Fox. "Fox! Where are you?" Kestrel shrieked. She flew under the bridge to look. But she couldn't see him. She sped back to tell the other animals.

Mole began to sob. "We've lost Fox. We've lost our leader."

Badger looked grim. "Then we must go on," he announced. "We can't remain here."

"But supposing Fox comes back?" Mole protested.

"If Fox is alive," Badger said wearily, "he'll find us. And I know he would want us to continue. So, get ready, everyone." Badger had assumed command.

Toad led the animals on through fields. "Nice springy grass just like I remember, mateys," he said as he hopped along. "We've come a long way."

"It's a long way from Fox, too," sobbed Mole.

Fox was very much alive. He had clambered from the driftwood into the back of a small boat. The boat sailed under the bridge and headed for a lock.

Once in the lock the water level rose. Fox peeped out. He could see a forest of human legs. Hands pointed at him. There were shouts.

"Look. A fox!"

"How did he get there?"

Fox was frightened. The boat rose higher still on the water. He made a tremendous leap, landing on the lock side. He dashed through the throng of astonished humans and reached the towpath.

Fox loped along the river bank, carefully avoiding passers-by. He knew the river would eventually lead him back to where he and his friends were parted. He ran a long way and then paused for a rest.

A horse stood in a neighbouring field under a shady tree.

"Mind if I join you?" Fox called.

"Please do," said the horse. "I don't normally see foxes around in broad daylight. Especially in hunting country."

Fox looked alarmed. "Hunting?"

"Yes. Lots of it round here. I shouldn't hang about in the open, if I were you."

"Don't worry, I won't," said Fox. "Just get my breath back. And thanks for the tip."

Fox trotted on, looking for a safe resting-place. Under a hedge he found the entrance to an empty den and crept inside. Unknown to Fox, a vixen, the den's owner, was watching him. She followed him in.

Fox jumped up, startled. "I'm sorry –" he began.

"It's all right," said Vixen. "You're welcome to rest. But I was about to go hunting. Will you come?"

"Gladly, after a rest. I'm famished."

While they hunted, Fox told Vixen about his friends, the Oath and their Journey. "And now I'm trying to find them again," he explained. "Although I wish I could stay with you," he added. "You're wonderful."

"You mustn't desert your friends, you're their leader," the Vixen answered. But she was flattered. "I'll come with you until you find them." Fox was heartened. "I need to pick up their trail. Perhaps the neighbourhood wildlife has a clue."

An owl had seen the party pass. He gave Fox news.

"Led by a badger?" Fox was delighted.

"They can't be far ahead," said Vixen.

They set off. Fox soon found the scent.

But later on this split into two trails. Fox was puzzled.

"Only one thing to do," said Vixen. "You follow one and I the other. Then, if you find you're on the wrong track, run back to join me. I'll do likewise."

Meanwhile Fox's friends had plodded uphill to a spinney from where they could view the surrounding countryside. Suddenly they were shaken by the awful sounds of the Hunt.

"I hope no foxes are about," said Mole.

The trail Vixen followed led nowhere. She turned tail, eager to rejoin Fox, but suddenly she heard the Hunt approaching and was terrified. She ran into a wood, zigzagging through the trees and diving through bushes, hoping to slow up the pursuing hounds. Fox, who was tracking his friends uphill, watched her flight.

"Run, Vixen, run!"

He saw the Hunt was gaining on her and galloped back towards her, intending to confuse the hounds and draw them after himself.

Up on the hill the other animals were watching, horror-struck.

"It's our Fox," groaned Toad.

They saw the hounds split into two packs, some following Fox and some Vixen.

"He's sacrificing himself", Badger muttered, "for the other animal."

Fox was leading the hounds back towards the hill. They began to ascend it. His friends saw the dogs approach.

"We must make our stand," said Badger. "Remember the Oath."

The Master of the Hunt saw the confusion. He called off the hounds who were following Fox, and the Hunt regrouped on Vixen's track. The exhausted Fox reached his friends.

"Fox! You're safe," said Badger. "They're after the other animal."

"I've failed her," Fox panted.

The animals were agog. "Who?"

"The vixen. She's my friend."

Vixen had sensed where Fox was and was heading for him.

"Come on, come on!" he encouraged her.

Vixen stumbled. Fox gasped. The Master's horse was almost on her. The man raised his whip to strike her back into the hounds' jaws. But Adder, hiding in the long grass, raised herself and buried her fangs in the horse's near leg. The horse reared in pain.

The Master was thrown to the ground. He yelled in agony. Vixen scrambled up and escaped into the spinney. The animals surrounded her. Kestrel cried, "The Hunt's called off. They're going!"

Adder was acclaimed as the heroine of the hour.
   "I was only saving my own skin," she protested. But she didn't fool anyone.

Fox and Vixen nuzzled one another. "You risked your life for me," she whispered. "How could we ever be parted now?"
   Fox was overjoyed.
   "Welcome, my dear," said Badger. "You're one of us now."

"We must move from here to a safer place," Fox said. "Kestrel, will you scout ahead?"

The bird flew high and returned with news. "There's a deserted quarry," she said, "and it's fenced round. We'd be more secure in there."

They set off for the quarry. Mole dug a hole under the fence so that everyone could pass underneath. Inside they found a large pond by which a heron was fishing.

"How do you do? My name's Whistler," he said. "It's my wing, you see." He showed them how a bullet had punctured it. "The air goes straight through it and makes a whistle." He demonstrated.

"We noticed you fishing," said Vixen.

"Yes, I've gathered quite a pile," Whistler replied. "Would you care to share it?"

While the animals ate, Whistler heard the story of their trek to the Nature Reserve.

"I'd like to join you," said Whistler, "if I may? It's very lonely here."

"You'd have to take the Oath," Adder hissed.

"He can do so with Vixen, who should also take it," Owl pointed out.

"I'd be glad to," said Vixen.

So the party now had two new members. The animals rested for a while in the peace of the quarry, but then the journey had to continue. Kestrel scouted ahead and discovered a fresh hazard – a motorway with six lanes of traffic.

"We've no choice," said Fox grimly. "We *have* to cross it. White Deer Park is on the other side."

Fox saw that the traffic in one direction was stationary, while in the other it continued to roar along. In the centre of the two flows was a strip of grass.

"We must help one another," said Fox. "Remember the Oath. The nearest cars aren't moving, so we could thread our way through those to the halfway point."

The animals crept to the roadside. Fox led the way with Toad and Weasel. They crawled between the cars and reached the central reservation.

Eventually all the animals stood together in the middle, choking in the exhaust fumes. For the moment they were stuck fast.

Whistler landed amongst them. "Can I help?" he asked. One by one he carried the smaller animals across to the far side.

At the same time a gap appeared in the moving traffic. Vixen saw the opportunity. "Run now!" she cried.

They dashed across to join the smaller animals but the noise of the traffic was too much for the hedgehogs. They tried to hide under the cars and rolled themselves up. It was the worst thing they could have done.

"Poor hedgehogs," Fox murmured. "They didn't stand a chance."

Only Adder had refused to cross the road at all. Owl flew back to find her. "You won't get me committing suicide," Adder hissed.

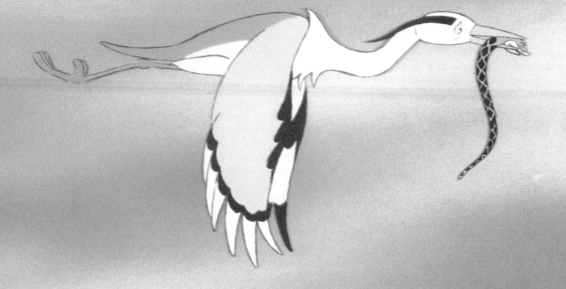

But before Adder knew what was happening Whistler landed beside them and snatched her up. The animals laughed as Adder arrived on the other side, dangling from Whistler's beak, hissing furiously.

On the last stage of their trek the party travelled with renewed hope. Only fields separated them from their goal. One vast field consisted entirely of young cabbages. Nothing else grew there. It was completely silent and eerie. The animals didn't feel comfortable. They hardly spoke.

"There's something odd here," said Fox, sniffing the ground.

"Why is it that, apart from ourselves, there's no living creatures to be seen here?"

Owl soon discovered the answer.

"You're on poisoned land," she announced.

"Of course," Fox muttered. "That smell! The cabbages have been sprayed!"

"But how can humans eat the cabbages?" Hare demanded. "Won't they die?"

"Perhaps slowly," Owl answered wisely.

"Let's get out of here *now*," said Fox.

So they hurried on their way.

As they neared the Park, the animals felt a warm glow in one another's company.

"It's the Oath which has made our dreams possible," said Mrs Vole. "It's changed us. Whoever would have thought a fox could be friends with a hare? We must keep the Oath in our new home and pass it on to our children. Then the spirit of our journey will last forever."

The leader of the White Deer herd, the Great Stag, stood ready to welcome them. Toad led the animals in.

"I've looked forward to this day," said the Stag. "News of your adventures reached us long ago. Here you can live free from interference from humankind. Welcome to White Deer Park!"